About this Book

In **Fish on a Walk,** Muggenthaler's richly detailed illustrations offer nearly endless possibilities for storytelling. At the bottom of each illustration there are just two words, which serve as a jumping off point for the reader's own responses. How do the words relate to the picture they accompany and what stories do we think each picture might tell? It's all there for the reader to decide.

Once upon a time there was a fish. This fish went for a walk with **his** friend or maybe it was **her** friend? Or perhaps the two fish are related in some way? Since it's about to rain, they put up their umbrella, though perhaps they have it to protect them from the sun? A group of bugs looks up at the fish with surprise. Is it because it's unusual to see fish taking a walk, or is it because one of them is whistling? The words accompanying this picture are "usual - unusual," and the question that is being asked is, what seems normal and what strange? The answer isn't as simple as it might seem, and this is where things get exciting, since the discussion that develops around the picture and the stories that get told might be just about anything.

A charming, thought-provoking book to explore again and again!

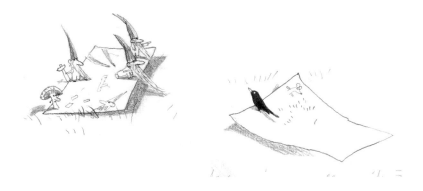

www.enchantedlionbooks.com

First American Edition published in 2011 by
Enchanted Lion Books, 20 Jay Street, Studio M-18, Brooklyn, NY 11201
Originally published in Germany by Mixtvision Verlag, München © 2010 as
Als die Fische spazieren gingen… by Eva Muggenthaler
All rights reserved under International and Pan-American Copyright Conventions
ISBN 978-1-59270-116-2
Printed in August 2011 in China by Leo Paper Group.

Fish On A Walk

Written and Illustrated by Eva Muggenthaler

ENCHANTED LION BOOKS
NEW YORK

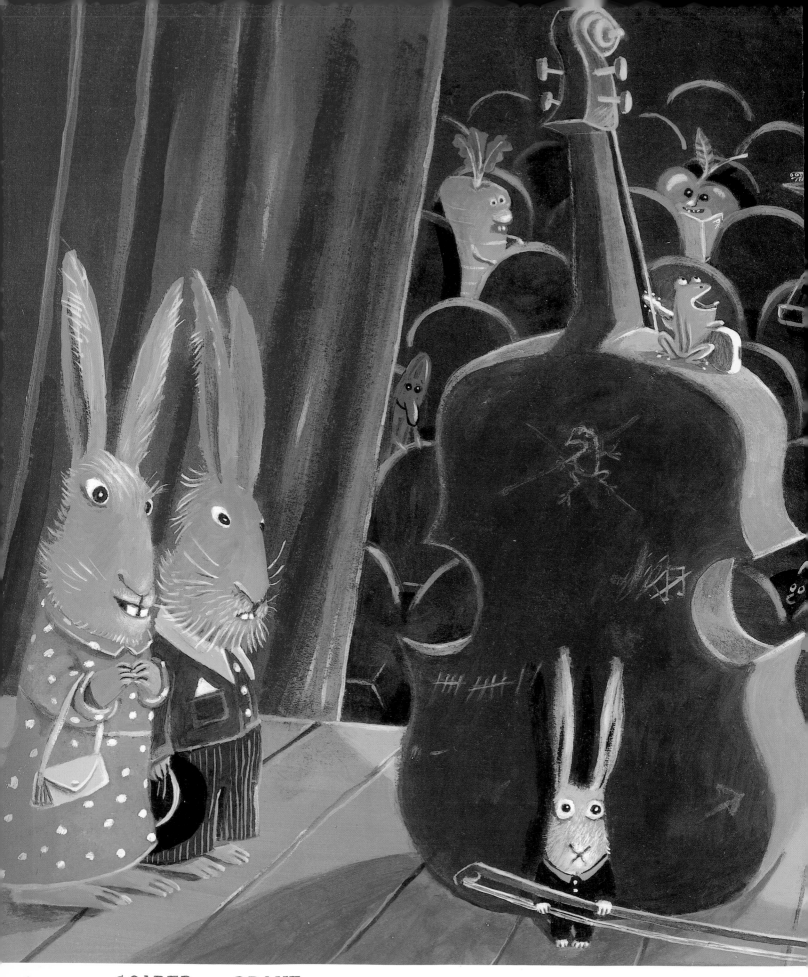

SCARED – BRAVE

ALONE – TOGETHER

10   HAPPY — SAD

12   CRANKY – KIND

14   USUAL – UNUSUAL

16   JEALOUS - ACCEPTING

18   RUDE – FRIENDLY

SAME – DIFFERENT

WILD – POLITE

LAZY – HARDWORKING

TRICKY — TRUTHFUL

READY FOR FUN - READY FOR BED